PUFFIN BOOKS

The Slippers that Answered Back

Gyles Brandreth has had a varied career, working in the theatre, publishing and television before becoming the Member of Parliament for the City of Chester in 1992. He is the author of a large number of books on a wide range of topics, and once featured in *The Guinness Book of Records* for making the longest ever after-dinner speech – twelve and a half hours! With his wife, Michele, he is the founder of the Teddy Bear Museum in Stratford-upon-Avon, and he is Vice-President of the National Playing Fields Association, the charity that protects and improves playgrounds and play space throughout the United Kingdom.

Some other books by Gyles Brandreth

THE MERMAID AT No. 13
THE WITCH AT NO. 13
THE MONSTERS AT NO. 13

THE SLIPPERS THAT TALKED
THE SLIPPERS THAT ANSWERED BACK

GYLES BRANDRETH

The Slippers That Answered Back

Illustrated by Annie Horwood

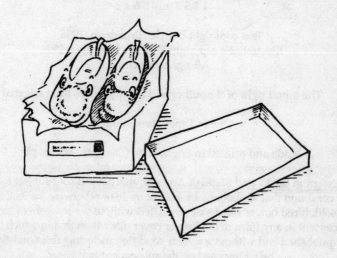

PUFFIN BOOKS

PUFFIN BOOKS

Published by the Penguin Group
Penguin Books Ltd, 27 Wrights Lane, London W8 5TZ, England
Penguin Putnam Inc., 375 Hudson Street, New York,
New York 10014, USA
Penguin Books Australia Ltd, Ringwood, Victoria, Australia
Penguin Books Canada Ltd, 10 Alcorn Avenue, Toronto,
Ontario, Canada M4V 3B2
Penguin Books (NZ) Ltd, Private Bag 102902, NSMC,
Auckland, New Zealand

On the worldwide web at: www.penguin.com

Penguin Books Ltd, Registered Offices: Harmondsworth,
Middlesex, England

First published by Viking 1996
Published in Puffin Books 1999
1 3 5 7 9 10 8 6 4 2

Set in Times New Roman

Made and printed in England by Clays Ltd, St Ives plc

British Library Cataloguing in Publication Data
A CIP catalogue record for this book is available from
the British Library

ISBN 0–140–37833–2

Contents

Contents

The Amazing Slippers

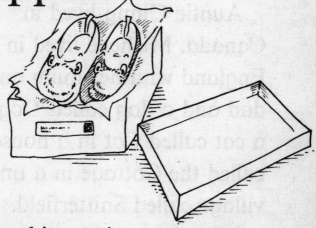

Something quite extraordinary had happened to Michelle on her seventh birthday. Her Auntie Ginny had sent her a pair of slippers.

They weren't ordinary slippers, of course. They were magic slippers. One was red and one was blue. They had funny faces and they could talk.

Auntie Ginny lived in Canada. Michelle lived in England with her mum and her dad and a dog called Dog and a cat called Cat in a house called the Cottage in a tiny village called Snitterfield.

Michelle loved her home and her mum and her dad. Even though she had never met her, she also loved Auntie Ginny. She loved Dog a lot. She *had* loved Cat too, until the day last summer when Cat got into her bedroom and ate her

goldfish (who was called
Willie). When Cat ate Willie –
which was a natural thing for
a cat to do, but horrid all the
same – Michelle said to
herself, "I will never ever
EVER talk to Cat again."
And she hadn't.

Most of all, and best of all,
Michelle loved her slippers.
She kept them in the cupboard
in her bedroom, wrapped in
tissue-paper inside a
cardboard box, and every
day, as soon as she got in
from school, she ran upstairs
to check they were all right.

Dog always ran upstairs with her. Dog was Michelle's best friend. She told him all her secrets. And because Dog was a dog, he was very trustworthy and he never told those secrets to anyone.

Of course, the magic slippers were Michelle's biggest secret. Dog knew all about them. Tiggy Smith knew about them too. Michelle didn't like Tiggy. They were in the same class and, one day, when Michelle had taken her slippers to school hidden in her lunch-box, Tiggy had tried to run off with them.

Tiggy was tall and thin and had short, curly red hair and freckles. Michelle had long fair hair and Tiggy had pulled it once. "I hate boys with red hair," said Michelle. "They look stupid."

Tiggy wasn't stupid. He was rather clever, even if he wasn't always very nice. He lived in a large house at the other end of the village with his mother and his grandfather and a mina bird called Fred. Fred was famous throughout Snitterfield because he could talk. At least, he could say "Hello" and "Goodbye" and

"Who's a pretty boy, then?"

Michelle's slippers could say much more than that. They could say anything they liked. In fact, they didn't say a lot because of the special way their magic worked. They only talked to you if you were ill.

Who's a pretty boy, then?

TIGG

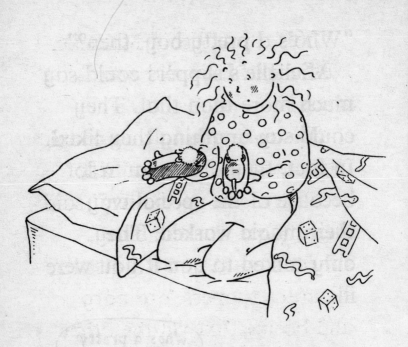

On the day that the slippers
arrived at the Cottage,
Michelle was in bed with flu.
"You must be sick," said the
red slipper, after he had
introduced himself and
explained that his name was
Left.

"Yes, I am," said Michelle, "just a bit. How did you guess?"

"We can only talk to people when they're ill," said Left.

"When you get better," said Right (that was the blue slipper's name), "we'll just be ordinary slippers, ordinary and boring, like all the other slippers in the world."

"But right now," said Left, "we're amazing!" And so they were.

The trouble was, of course, that as soon as Michelle got better, the slippers shut up.

For weeks and weeks they

said nothing at all. Every day, after school, Michelle and Dog would run upstairs and Dog would guard the door while Michelle opened the cardboard box.

"Now you two," she would say, putting her hands inside the slippers and holding them close to her face, "what have you got to say for yourselves?"

The slippers said nothing.

"Please," said Michelle, "please, please, please, please. PLEASE say something."

The slippers said nothing. For two months, three weeks

and four days, the slippers did
not let out so much as a
squeak.

"I'm fed up with you two
not talking to me," said
Michelle very crossly, and
instead of wrapping them up
in the tissue-paper and putting

them back in the box, she threw them both on to the floor.

"Ouch!" said Left.

"That hurt!" said Right.

"What did you say?" gasped Michelle.

"I said 'That hurt!'" said the blue slipper.

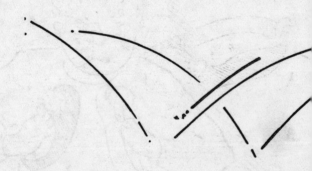

"I thought that's what you said," laughed Michelle. "That's wonderful!"

"It may be wonderful for you," said Left, "but it was pretty painful for us."

"I didn't mean that," said Michelle, picking up the pair of slippers and giving them a

big hug. "I meant it's wonderful that you're talking again."

Right sighed and smiled. "First she chucks us on the floor, next she tells us we're wonderful."

Left chuckled. "She's some crazy mixed-up kid, that's for sure!"

"Say, Michelle," said Right, looking up at the seven-year-old girl who hadn't felt so happy since her birthday. "What's wrong with you this time?"

"What do you mean?" asked Michelle.

"How do you feel?" said
Left. "Is it flu again? Or have
you got the measles?"

"I'm fine," said Michelle,
thinking that in all her seven-
and-a-quarter years she had
never felt better than she felt
right now.

"I don't get it," said Right, looking puzzled. "We slippers can only talk when there's someone sick about. If it isn't you, Michelle, who is it?"

"Woof!" barked Dog very softly.

Poor Dog!

"It must be Dog!" cried Michelle. "What's wrong with him?"

"Let's take a look," said the red slipper. "Sit, doggie."

Dog sat and gave a little growl. With one hand Michelle patted Dog gently on the head, and with the other she held up the pair of slippers

so that they could take a
closer look.

"He's a handsome animal,"
said the blue slipper,
admiringly. "He's got a lovely
shiny coat and beautiful
bright eyes."

"His nose is wet and cold,"
said Michelle.

"That's good," said Right.

"But look at his mouth,"
said Left.

"What's wrong with his
mouth?" asked Michelle,
anxiously.

"I'm not sure," said Left.
"It looks a little swollen,
that's all."

"Woof!" barked Dog.

"Closer, please," instructed Right, as Michelle held the slippers up to Dog's jaw. "Can you see what I see?"

"No," said Michelle.

"Yes," said Left. "He's been stung by a wasp."

"Poor Dog!" cried Michelle.

"Woof!" barked Dog.

"I bet he's been out in the garden chasing butterflies and bees," said Right,

"Woof, woof!" barked Dog, wagging his tail.

"What shall we do?" asked

Michelle, putting her arm around her pet.

"Let's play a game," suggested Left.

Michelle looked shocked. "You want to play a game when poor Dog's so ill? Shouldn't we be taking him to the vet?"

"It's not that serious," said Right. "If we play a game it will take his mind off it."

"Woof, woof!" barked Dog again, wagging his tail even faster.

"You see," said Left, "he agrees. What shall we play?"

"How about Hunt the

Slipper?" suggested Right. "Do you play that over here? In Canada we play it all the time."

"What happens?" asked Michelle.

"You close your eyes and count to ten," explained Right. "While you've got your eyes shut, Dog hides us somewhere. When you open your eyes you've got to find us. When you've found us, you've won!"

For the next hour, Dog forgot all about the wasp sting as he and Michelle and Left and Right played Hunt

the Slipper. Michelle was
better at finding than hiding
and Dog was better at hiding
than finding. First he hid the
slippers under Michelle's bed,
then he hid them under her
duvet. Then he climbed from

her bed on to her chest of
drawers and managed to hide
the slippers on top of her
cupboard.

Michelle was sitting on the
edge of her bed with her eyes

...Six, seven,
eight...

closed counting to ten and
Dog had just hidden the
slippers inside the waste-paper
basket by the window when
the door to Michelle's room
burst open and in came Mum.

"Are you ready?"

"Ready for what?" asked
Michelle, opening her eyes.

"Ready to go to Gramps,"
said Mum. "It's Thursday.
You hadn't forgotten, had
you?"

Michelle had forgotten. On
Thursdays Michelle and her
Mum always drove over to
the next village to have tea
with Mum's dad. Sometimes

they stayed the night. Michelle liked staying with Gramps because he had a rabbit called Rory, who was allowed to run around the house like a cat, and a duck called Emerald who laid gigantic eggs that Gramps boiled for their tea.

"Hurry up now," said Mum. "I'm going to start the car."

"Coming!" said Michelle, and as soon as her mum was out of the room, she called out to the slippers, "I've got to go now, but wherever you're hiding I'll find you tomorrow. Dog will keep you company, won't you, Dog?"

"Woof!" barked Dog.

"Cheerio!" called Right from inside the waste-paper basket.

"See you!" said Left.

"'Bye now!" shouted

Michelle as she clattered down the stairs.

On Friday afternoon, as soon as Michelle got in from school, she collected Dog from the kitchen and ran upstairs

with him to her room. "Now where have you hidden those slippers?"

Dog growled.

"Don't worry," said Michelle. "I'll find them." She looked everywhere. She looked on top of the bed and under it, inside the cupboard and behind it, under the rug and around the radiator and behind the curtains. She even looked inside the waste-paper basket. She couldn't find the magic slippers anywhere.

"All right," she said. "I give up. Where are you?"

Dog gave a little whimper,

but there was no sound from any slippers.

"Come on," said Michelle, "you win. Tell me where you are!"

Dog growled and wandered over to the waste-paper basket.

"They aren't there, Dog," said Michelle. "Why won't they tell us where they're hiding?"

"Woof!" barked Dog.

"Of course," said Michelle, going over to Dog and taking a close look at him. "I know what's happened. You're better, aren't you?"

"Woof!" barked Dog, wagging his tail.

Just then, Mum put her
head around the door.

"Mum," said Michelle,
"have you seen my slippers?"

"Yes," said Mum, "I found
them in your waste-paper
basket this morning."

"Where did you put them?"

"I gave them to Mrs Andrews," said Mum in a matter-of-fact sort of way. "She was collecting jumble for her stall at the church fair and, since you'd thrown them away, I thought you wouldn't mind if I gave them to a good cause."

Michelle didn't know what to say, so she burst into tears.

Catch the Rat

At ten o'clock on Saturday
morning, Michelle and Dog
were standing at the front of a
very long queue outside
Snitterfield church hall. As the
church clock struck ten, Mr
Andrews, the vicar, opened
the doors and said, "Welcome
to our autumn fair,
everybody."

Everybody surged past the
vicar and into the hall. They
all seemed to know where they
were going except for Michelle
and Dog. Mrs Griggs was
aiming for the cake stall. Mr
Griggs made his way towards
the second-hand books. Miss

Hobart, who was very old and very bent, wanted to buy some raffle tickets and then find somewhere quiet to sit. Her sister, who was also called Miss Hobart but wasn't quite so old and bent, wanted to know if there was a fortune-teller at the fair this year.

"I'm afraid not," said Mr Andrews, "but we've got a talking mina bird, and a game where you have to throw wooden hoops over bottles of tomato ketchup!"

Michelle and Dog pushed their way through the crowd in search of the magic slippers. Almost at once they came across a small table piled high with boots and shoes.

"This is it," thought Michelle. "Excuse me," she said to the old gentleman who was standing behind the table, "do you have any slippers for sale?"

"Boots and shoes I have," said the old gentleman, "and a pair of skis and an old electric toaster, but I'm afraid a pair of slippers is the one thing I haven't got. I've got Aladdin's lamp, if that's any use to you?"

Michelle's eyes began to

light up. "Is it really Aladdin's lamp?" she asked.

"Well, er, I'm not sure about that," said the old gentleman. "It was young Tiggy Smith who brought it in. He said it was Aladdin's lamp, but I wouldn't like to guarantee it."

"Is Tiggy Smith here?" asked Michelle, thinking to herself, "I hate Tiggy Smith. I hate boys with red hair."

"Yes," said the old gentleman, "he's with his grandfather's mina bird, up on the stage by the second-hand clothes stall."

Michelle looked in the direction the old gentleman was pointing and there, on the small wooden stage at the far end of the church hall, was a long table covered with old clothes. Mrs Andrews was standing at one end holding a gigantic jar of sweets. Tiggy

Smith was at the other end with a big wooden hammer in his hand.

Michelle and Dog pushed through the crowd until they reached the stage and found the four narrow steps leading up to it.

"Hello, Michelle," said Mrs
Andrews cheerily. "Guess the
number of sweets in the jar
and you win the lot!"

"Woof!" barked Dog who
was thinking that a few sweets
were just what the vet would
have ordered for a dog

recovering from a wasp sting.

"And thank you for those lovely slippers," continued Mrs Andrews. "I loved their happy faces. It was jolly kind of you and your mum to let us have them for my stall."

Suddenly Michelle's head prickled and she felt quite out of breath. "Where are they?" she asked.

"I've sold them," said Mrs Andrews, happily. "Tiggy Smith bought them for 50p. He got a bargain, don't you think?"

Michelle didn't know what to think. All she knew was

that Tiggy Smith, horrid,
stupid Tiggy Smith, Tiggy
Smith who pulled her hair and
stuck his tongue out at her,
had got her magic slippers
and she had to get them back.
Michelle ran along the front
of the stage. She ran so
quickly she almost fell off.

At the other end, Tiggy
Smith had a small crowd
standing round him. Fred the
mina bird was in this cage
cawing, "Goodbye, hello,
who's a pretty boy, then?"
Tiggy Smith was standing by
a blackboard that had a long
cardboard tube fixed to it. In

one hand he was holding the
magic slippers, in the other he
had a wooden mallet.

"Roll up! Roll up!" he was
calling. "Only 10p a go to
catch the rat. If you trap him
you win 20p."

"What happens?" asked a
small boy standing right at
the front of the group.

"I drop a rat down the tube," explained Tiggy. "You have the hammer and if you manage to whack him as he comes out the other end you win the prize. It's easy!"

"Where are the rats?" asked the small boy.

"Here they are!" cried Tiggy, waving the two magic slippers in the air. "You take the hammer and I'll drop the slippers down the tube."

"Don't you dare!" screamed Michelle, pushing past the small boy and trying to grab the slippers from Tiggy's hand. "Give them to me!"

"They're mine!" called
Tiggy, holding the slippers as
high above his head as he
could and running quickly
behind the table.

"Come here!" shouted
Michelle chasing after him.

"Woof!" barked Dog.

The small boy started
crying and Mrs Andrews

called out, "Stop it! Stop it, you two!" But it was too late. Just as Michelle and Dog were about to catch up with him, Tiggy Smith reached the top of the steps at the side of the stage, slipped, lost his balance and fell, thump, thump, THUMP, down the stairs.

"Oh dear," said Mrs Andrews.

"I'm sorry," said Michelle.

"I think he's broken a leg," said Left in a loud whisper.

"Who said that?" asked Mrs Andrews, bending over Tiggy.

"I did," said Michelle quickly.

Tiggy Smith groaned.

"Does it hurt a lot?" asked
Mrs Andrews.

"Yes," said Tiggy, trying
hard not to cry.

"What shall we do?" asked
Michelle, picking up the magic
slippers from where they had

fallen on the floor.

"Don't move him," said Right.

"Call an ambulance," said Left.

Mrs Andrews looked puzzled. "Who said that?"

"We did!" said the slippers.

"I did!" said Michelle.

"Woof!" barked Dog.

"Whoever it was," said Mrs Andrews, scratching her head, "it's a very good idea."

Poor Tiggy!

There was a telephone just inside the entrance to the church hall. Mr Andrews, the vicar, dialled 999.

"Emergency services," said the voice at the other end of the line. "Police, fire, ambulance, which service do you require?"

"We need an ambulance, please," said the vicar. "There's been an accident at Snitterfield church hall. A boy has fallen off the stage and we think he's broken his leg."

Exactly eight minutes later the ambulance arrived. Three paramedics jumped out, ran into the church hall and pushed their way through the crowd. The one in charge was called Jo. Michelle didn't like the look of her. She had freckles and red hair.

"What's the problem then?" asked Jo, bending over to take a closer look at Tiggy who was still lying on the floor and looking very uncomfortable indeed.

"He's broken his leg!" hissed Left rather loudly.

"Who said that?" said Jo, turning round sharply.

"I did," said Michelle,

quickly hiding the slippers
behind her back.

"Let's ask the patient, shall
we?" said Jo, and she gave
Michelle a very unfriendly
look.

"I think I've twisted my
ankle," whispered poor Tiggy.

"He's broken his leg," hissed
Left from behind Michelle's
back. "Any fool can tell that."

"Are you a doctor?" asked
Jo, looking at Michelle fiercely.

"No," stammered Michelle.

"But she knows a broken leg
when she sees one," snorted
Left.

Jo stared hard at Michelle.

"Your lips didn't move. Are
you some kind of ventriloquist?"

"No, it wasn't me,"
spluttered Michelle. "It was
the slip–"

"It was the bird!" interrupted
Right loudly.

"Who's a pretty boy, then?"
squawked Fred.

"I've had enough of this," said Jo. "We need to get this lad to hospital and no more messing about."

Jo supervised while the two other paramedics unrolled a stretcher and carefully lifted Tiggy Smith on to it. He screwed up his face and he winced, but he didn't cry.

"Goodbye, hello, goodbye!" squawked the mina bird.

"We'll take Fred home," said Mrs Andrews, "and we'll let your mother know what's happened. She'll come and find you at the hospital."

"Thanks," whispered Tiggy.

"Can I have my slippers back?"

Michelle tried to hide the slippers up her jumper.

"What are you up to now, young lady?" asked Jo, turning to Michelle and raising her eyebrows suspiciously.

"They're my slippers!" said Michelle firmly.

"They're mine!" said Tiggy.

"Let's have a look at them," said Jo sternly.

Michelle held out the red and blue slippers. "They're mine," she repeated. "They were a birthday present from my Auntie Ginny in Canada."

"They're mine now," said Tiggy. "I paid 50p for them."

"He can't wear slippers," hissed Left. "He's got a broken leg."

"He certainly can't wear two slippers at the moment," said Mrs Andrews, trying to be helpful. "Why don't you have one slipper each?"

"No!" chorused four voices all at once.

"Good idea!" said Jo and she yanked the red slipper out of Michelle's hand and gave it to Tiggy Smith.

"Help!" shouted Left as the

paramedics lifted Tiggy's
stretcher off the floor. "Help!"

"Come back!" called Right
as loudly as he could. "Come
back!" He went on shouting,
but his voice grew fainter and
fainter as the paramedics
made their way through the
hall to the door.

"I'm sure that girl's a ventriloquist," muttered Jo, narrowing her eyes and taking a last good look at Michelle as she followed the stretcher out to the ambulance.

"Who's a pretty boy then?" squawked Fred, as Mr and Mrs Andrews carried his cage through the village on their way to tell Tiggy Smith's mother the bad news about Tiggy's accident.

"There's something odd about those slippers," said Mrs Andrews, "that's for sure."

Michelle felt very sorry for

herself as she walked home to the Cottage with Dog's lead in one hand and her blue slipper in the other.

"It isn't fair, is it, Dog?" she said. Dog barked. Dog agreed.

"What are we going to do?" she asked the blue slipper, holding him up so she could see his face. Right smiled an encouraging smile and made big eyes at her, but he didn't say a word.

"Oh dear," sighed Michelle. "I'm not ill and Dog's better and that means the slipper can't talk. This is terrible!"

"You look down in the
dumps," said Mum as soon as
she saw her. "Didn't you find
your slippers then?"

Michelle told Mum the
whole story – well, it wasn't
quite the whole story. Michelle
didn't tell her mother about
the slippers being magic
slippers because she knew her
mother wouldn't believe her.

"Poor Tiggy Smith," said Mum. "I think we'd better go and visit him in hospital, don't you?"

Michelle didn't want to visit Tiggy Smith anywhere, but she did want to rescue her other slipper, so she said, "Yes, please. Can we go after tea?"

Dog barked and wagged his tail. Right looked up at Michelle and, when he was sure Mum wasn't looking, he winked at her and his lips twitched. "He's trying to say something," thought Michelle. "What can it be?"

The Get Well Present

It was a little after six when Michelle and her blue slipper, Mum and Dog arrived at the hospital.

"That's better!" chuckled Right as they walked through the large main door.

"Ssh!" whispered Michelle.

"Sorry!" hissed Right.

"Can I help you?" asked a fierce-looking lady who was sitting behind a large desk just inside the front entrance. "At least she hasn't got red hair," thought Michelle.

"We've come to visit Tiggy Smith," said Mum. "We've

brought him a get well
present."

"You've just missed his
mother and grandfather," said
the fierce-looking lady. "They
brought a very noisy bird with
them. People shouldn't bring
animals into a hospital. Is
that a dog you've got there?"
she added, looking fiercer
than ever and peering at Dog
over the top of her glasses.

"Of course it's a dog," said
Right very loudly. "What did
you think it was, a
kangaroo?"

Michelle put her thumb over
Right's mouth.

The fierce-looking lady turned bright red. "What did you say?"

"I said, he's a dog," spluttered Michelle, "but we call him Kangaroo because he hops about so much."

Dog went "Woof!" and did his best to hop up and down.

"Whatever he's called," said the fierce-looking lady, "he can't come in here."

"That's all right," said Mum quickly. "I'll wait outside with Dog, and you go and say hello to Tiggy. Here's his get well present, and don't forget to give him the 50p."

Mum took Dog outside
while Michelle and the blue
slipper tried to find their way
to the children's ward. "It's
through the double doors,
turn left, take the second
corridor on the right and go
up the first flight of stairs,"
said the fierce-looking lady.
"You can't miss it."

Not surprisingly, Michelle and the slipper quickly lost their way. They didn't mind. Michelle liked exploring and Right was happy because, as he said, "in a hospital almost everybody is ill so I can talk as much as I like!"

They didn't find the stairs, but eventually they came

across a lift and took it to the first floor. As soon as they stepped out of the lift, they heard a voice they both recognised. It was singing, and singing very loudly.

"She wore an itsy-bitsy teeny-weeny yellow polka dot bikini!"

"That's Left," said Right. "It sounds as if they're having a party."

Michelle and the blue slipper pushed open the swing doors and went into the children's ward. It was a light, bright room with a large window and jolly pictures of dancing elephants painted on the walls. There were six beds in the room and there appeared to be a child in each one, sound asleep.

"What's going on?" said Michelle.

"Where's the party?" said Right.

"We thought you were a nurse," said Tiggy, opening one eye.

"Hello," said a little girl in bright yellow pyjamas who was in the bed next to Tiggy's. "When the nurse comes in we have to pretend we're asleep."

"Where's Left?" asked
Michelle.

"I'm here," came a voice
from behind Tiggy's head.
Tiggy sat up and pulled the
red slipper out from under his
pillow. "We've been playing
games and having a sing-

song," explained Left with a laugh. "We're having a great time. And the good news is that Tiggy hasn't broken his leg after all. It's just a sprained ankle and he's going home tomorrow."

"Tiggy," said Michelle, "I'm sorry you fell off the stage and hurt your ankle. I've brought you a present and 50p."

Michelle put the parcel and a 50p piece on the locker at the side of Tiggy's bed.

"Thanks," said Tiggy.

"Can I have my slipper back now?" asked Michelle.

"No!" said Tiggy, grabbing

hold of the red slipper. "He's mine!"

"That's not fair," said Michelle.

"Don't worry," whispered Right very quietly, "I've got a plan."

At that point a nurse put her head around the door and said, "Can we have a little less noise in here, please? This is a hospital not a playground."

"Excuse me," called Right.

"Did you say something?" said the nurse, coming into the ward and looking at Michelle.

"No," said Michelle,

"Yes," said Right, trying to sound as much like a seven-year-old girl as a Canadian slipper can. "Yes, nurse, can you help me?"

"But your lips aren't moving," said the nurse, looking very puzzled.

"I know," said Right quickly. "That's because I'm a crazy mixed-up kid. You see, I speak through my nose and I breathe through my mouth, like this."

Michelle was beginning to get the idea. She took a very large breath.

"See?" said Right, happily.

The nurse looked even more puzzled. "Are you sure you're feeling all right?" she asked.

Michelle took another big

breath. "No," said Right,
"I'm feeling rather hot. You
couldn't open the window,
could you?"

The nurse went over to the
large window and opened it.
"You stand here and get some
fresh air," she said. "I'll just
go and fetch a doctor."

Michelle went and stood by the open window while the nurse hurried off.

"Let's play another game," suggested Left as soon as the nurse had gone. "How about Pass the Parcel?"

"How do you play that?" asked the little girl in the bright yellow pyjamas.

"I'm the parcel," said Left, "and I get passed from bed to bed and whoever's holding me when the nurse comes back is out."

"Sounds great!" said Right.

"All right," said Tiggy, throwing the red slipper across

the room to the boy in the bed opposite him. The boy threw Left back to the girl in the bright yellow pyjamas and then she threw the slipper to the girl in the bed in the far corner.

"Me next!" called Michelle and the girl threw the slipper to her. As soon as Michelle caught the slipper, Left shouted, "Throw us out the window!" Michelle didn't stop to think. She did as she was told and threw Left and Right out of the open window.

At that moment the door to the ward swung open and the nurse reappeared.

"Doctor will be here in a moment," she said.

"I'm feeling better now, thanks very much," said Michelle quickly. "I think I'd better be going." And as fast as her legs would carry her, Michelle ran out of the ward, along the corridor, down the stairs and out of the hospital.

"What an odd girl," said the nurse, shaking her head. She went over to the window and as she began to close it she looked out and saw Michelle and her mum and Dog walking towards the hospital car park. "Am I imagining things or has that dog got a pair of slippers in his mouth?"

"They're my slippers," said Tiggy Smith.

"Are you sure?" said the nurse.

"I paid 50p for them," said Tiggy.

"What's that?" asked the nurse, looking at the 50p on

Tiggy's bedside locker. "And what's in the parcel you've got there?"

"I don't know," said Tiggy and then he began to unwrap the package that Michelle's mum had given her to give to Tiggy as a get well present. "I don't believe it," he gasped, as he pulled off the wrapping

paper and gazed down at a pair of brand new slippers. One was green and one was orange and they both had funny smiling faces.

In the car driving home from the hospital, Michelle sat in the back next to Dog with her magic slippers safely on her lap. "I hope Tiggy likes his get well present," said Michelle.

"He will," said Mum.

"Woof!" said Dog.

The slippers didn't say a word.

The Slippers That Talked

Gyles Brandreth

"Ordinary slippers might be boring," said the red slipper, "but we're not."

Michelle thinks that her seventh birthday is going to be the best ever. But it isn't – it is the worst. For a start, it's Sunday and her parents wake up late. There is no post and her presents are boring. Then Michelle is sick – and that's when the fun starts!

What looks like a boring old pair of slippers turns out to be the most exciting birthday present Michelle has ever had!

A perfect read for anyone who has ever had a birthday.

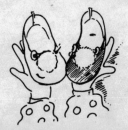

Also in Young Puffin

CLASS THREE AND THE BEANSTALK

Martin Waddell

A GIANT beanstalk and a BIG surprise!

Class Three's project on growing things
gets out of hand after they plant a packet
of Jackson's Giant Bean seeds. The
resulting beanstalk keeps growing...and
growing...and growing...
Wilbur Small is coming home! Everyone
is delighted and making great
preparations. All except for the Grice
family who are new and don't know what
all the fuss is about...

Fanny Witch and the Thunder Lizard

Jeremy Strong

"Oh dear, oh dear. Don't you see? That monster has eaten my Book of Spells. Eaten it!"

Everybody loves Fanny Witch, the schoolteacher, until she magics up a fully grown, live brontosaurus for the children, and the thunder lizard steals her Spell Book so she can't *un*magic the brontosaurus away.

When the boosnatch comes to the village and steals all the children, Fanny Witch has to come to the rescue!

DRAGON RIDE

Helen Cresswell

"I'm not joking, Dad," said Jilly. "I really, really want a dragon."

But only Mr Pink at the magic shop takes her seriously and helps her get a pet dragon. Soon all Jilly's dreams come true on her very own Dragon Ride.

Also in Young Puffin

There's a Troll at the Bottom of my Garden

Ann Jungman

I'm a troll, fol-de-rol,
I'm a troll, fol-de-rol,
I'm a troll, fol-de-rol,
And I'll eat you for my supper.

But the troll in this book doesn't like eating people, or goats. He likes eating ice-cream and he's very, very hungry. When Selima, Darren and Patrick find him crying in the garden shed they spend all their pocket money on ice-cream. But everything goes wrong when their parents find out . . .
or does it?

Find out how a troll becomes a good neighbour to everyone in Sebastopol Avenue, and how you can be one too!

READ MORE IN PUFFIN

For children of all ages, Puffin represents quality and variety – the very best in publishing today around the world.

For complete information about books available from Puffin – and Penguin – and how to order them, contact us at the appropriate address below. Please note that for copyright reasons the selection of books varies from country to country.

On the worldwide web: www.penguin.co.uk

In the United Kingdom: Please write to *Dept. EP, Penguin Books Ltd, Bath Road, Harmondsworth, West Drayton, Middlesex UB7 0DA*

In the United States: Please write to *Penguin Putnam inc., P.O. Box 12289, Dept B, Newark, New Jersey 07101-5289* or call 1-800-788-6262.

In Canada: Please write to *Penguin Books Canada Ltd, 10 Alcorn Avenue, Suite 300, Toronto, Ontario M4V 3B2*

In Australia: Please write to *Penguin Books Australia Ltd, P.O. Box 257, Ringwood, Victoria 3134*

In New Zealand: Please write to *Penguin Books (NZ) Ltd, Private Bag 102902, North Shore Mail Centre, Auckland 10*

In India: Please write to *Penguin Books India Pvt Ltd, 11 Panscheel Shopping Centre, Panscheel Park, New Delhi 110 017*

In the Netherlands: Please write to *Penguin Books Netherlands bv, Postbus 3507, NL-1001 AH Amsterdam*

In Germany: Please write to *Penguin Books Deutschland GmbH, Metzlerstrasse 26, 60594 Frankfurt am Main*

In Spain: Please write to *Penguin Books S. A., Bravo Murillo 19, 1° B, 28015 Madrid*

In Italy: Please write to *Penguin Italia s.r.l., Via Felice Casati 20, I–20124 Milano*

In France: Please write to *Penguin France S. A., 17 rue Lejeune, F–31000 Toulouse*

In Japan: Please write to *Penguin Books Japan, Ishikiribashi Building, 2–5–4, Suido, Bunkyo-ku, Tokyo 112*

In South Africa: Please write to *Longman Penguin Southern Africa (Pty) Ltd, Private Bag X08, Bertsham 2013*